CLEO
and the
COYOTE

by Elizabeth Levy

pictures by Diana Bryer

To Jason,
love,
Diana
Bryer
1999

HarperCollins*Publishers*

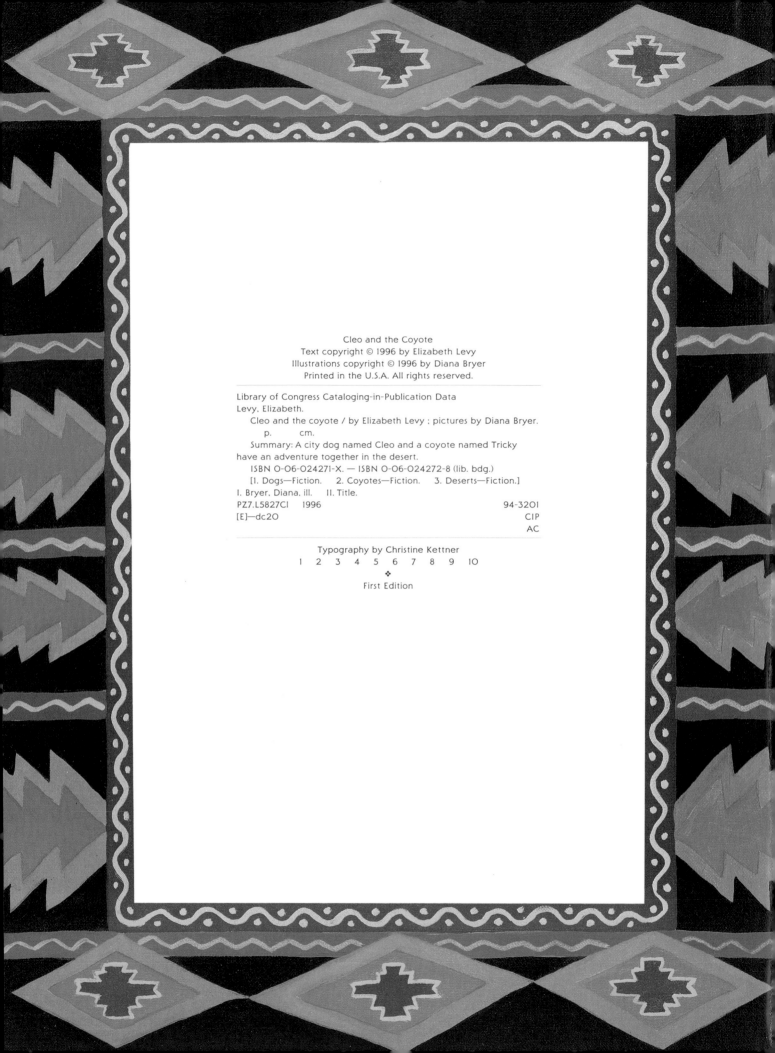

Cleo and the Coyote
Text copyright © 1996 by Elizabeth Levy
Illustrations copyright © 1996 by Diana Bryer
Printed in the U.S.A. All rights reserved.

Library of Congress Cataloging-in-Publication Data
Levy, Elizabeth.
  Cleo and the coyote / by Elizabeth Levy ; pictures by Diana Bryer.
     p.   cm.
  Summary: A city dog named Cleo and a coyote named Tricky
have an adventure together in the desert.
  ISBN 0-06-024271-X. — ISBN 0-06-024272-8 (lib. bdg.)
  [1. Dogs—Fiction.   2. Coyotes—Fiction.   3. Deserts—Fiction.]
I. Bryer, Diana, ill.   II. Title.
PZ7.L5827Cl   1996   94-3201
[E]—dc20   CIP
                                                                     AC

Typography by Christine Kettner
1   2   3   4   5   6   7   8   9   10
❖
First Edition

To Cleo and Gingy

—E.L.

To my three children,
Brian, Sara, and Simon

—D.B.

I never liked the word "owner." My first owner dumped me in the parking lot of Shea Stadium in Queens, New York. I lived on hot dogs. Hate the name. Love the taste.

One day after a baseball game, a boy grabbed me around the neck and hugged me. "Doggie," he said.

"Brilliant," I growled. He clung like mustard.

The boy's name was Martin. He and his mother took me home.

They named me Cleopatra because I was found in Queens. Cleopatra was a queen in Egypt. The name fits.

I was happy, well fed, and a little bored. It's hard to go from being a street dog to a lap dog.

Then one day Martin's mother took a cage out of the closet. I scooted under the bed. But I ended up in the baggage compartment of a noisy beast that Martin called an airplane. I chewed on my favorite squeak toy, a hot dog.

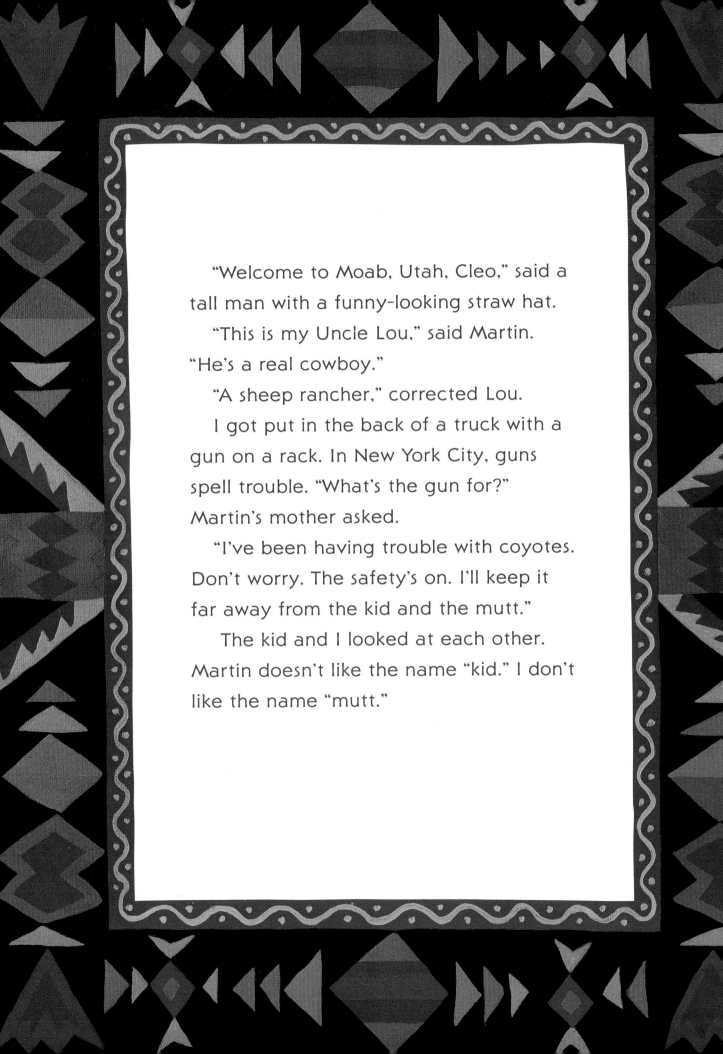

"Welcome to Moab, Utah, Cleo," said a
tall man with a funny-looking straw hat.

"This is my Uncle Lou," said Martin.
"He's a real cowboy."

"A sheep rancher," corrected Lou.

I got put in the back of a truck with a
gun on a rack. In New York City, guns
spell trouble. "What's the gun for?"
Martin's mother asked.

"I've been having trouble with coyotes.
Don't worry. The safety's on. I'll keep it
far away from the kid and the mutt."

The kid and I looked at each other.
Martin doesn't like the name "kid." I don't
like the name "mutt."

Lou made us hamburgers over an open fire for dinner. As we ate, the stars came out.

I fell asleep on the hard rock. I dreamed I was alone in the streets, hiding under a car from rats. I felt a rat shaking my leg.

"Cleo, it's me," whispered Martin. "The howling woke me." His fist was digging into my fur. He looked scared, so I licked his face.

I tried to tell him it was me, having a dogmare. But then I heard it too. *Ow-woo-ooooooo-owooooooo!* Someone was howling. And it *wasn't* me.

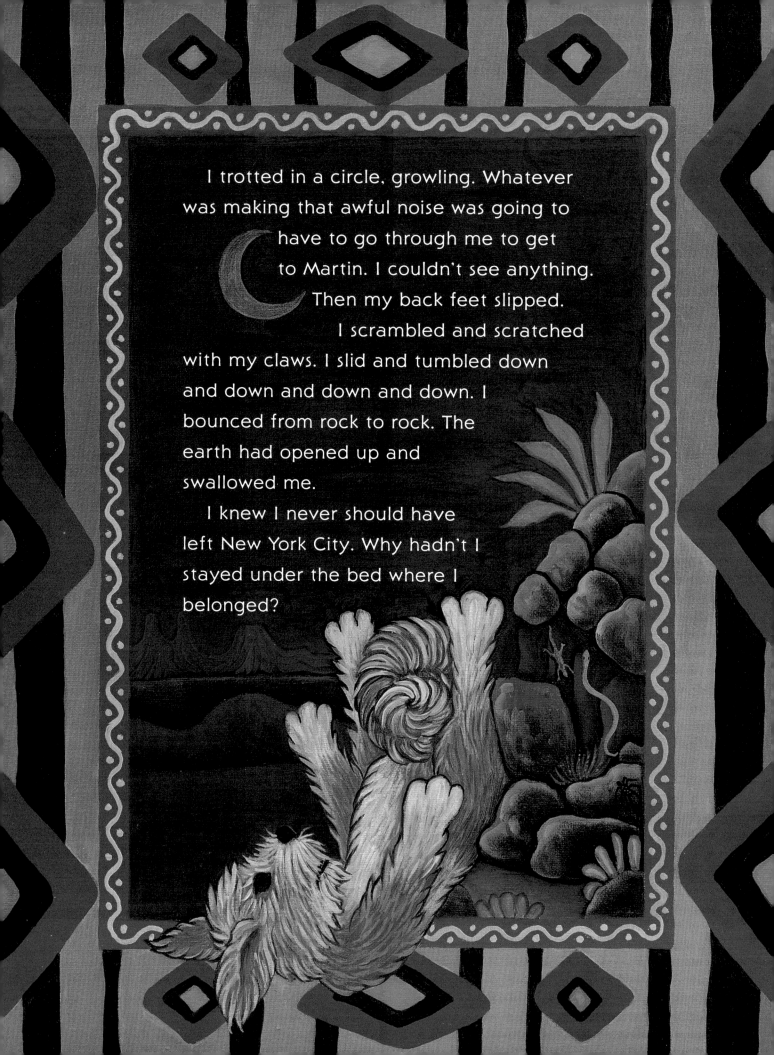

I trotted in a circle, growling. Whatever
was making that awful noise was going to
have to go through me to get
to Martin. I couldn't see anything.
Then my back feet slipped.
I scrambled and scratched
with my claws. I slid and tumbled down
and down and down and down. I
bounced from rock to rock. The
earth had opened up and
swallowed me.
I knew I never should have
left New York City. Why hadn't I
stayed under the bed where I
belonged?

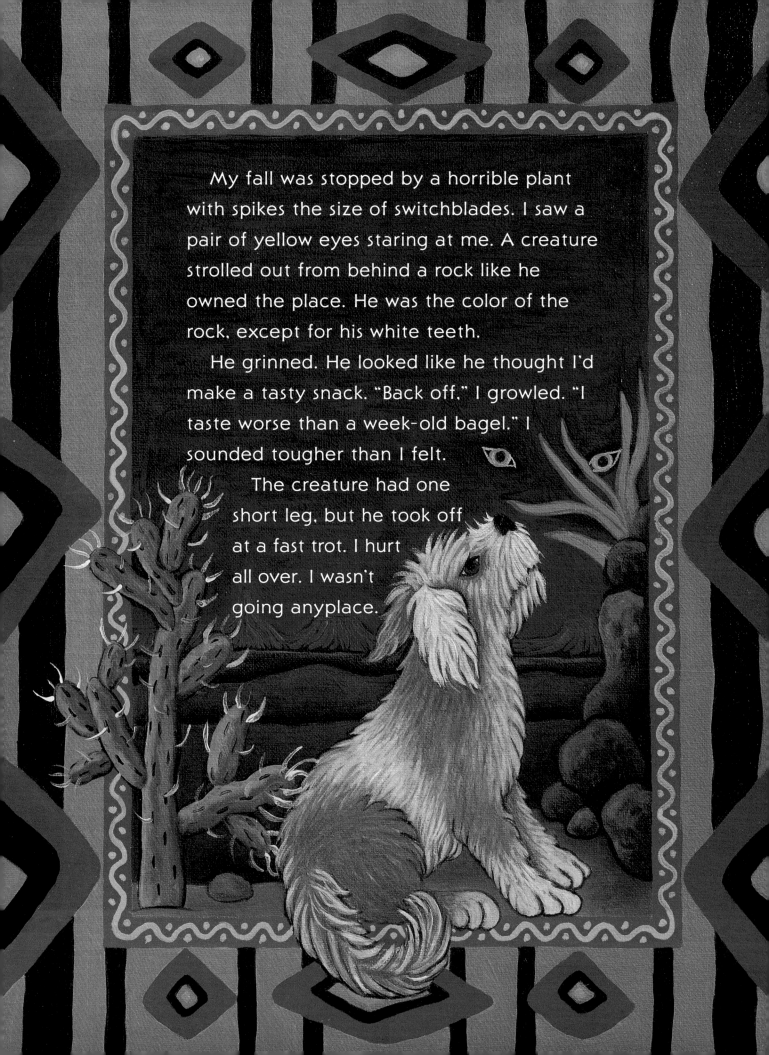

My fall was stopped by a horrible plant with spikes the size of switchblades. I saw a pair of yellow eyes staring at me. A creature strolled out from behind a rock like he owned the place. He was the color of the rock, except for his white teeth.

He grinned. He looked like he thought I'd make a tasty snack. "Back off." I growled. "I taste worse than a week-old bagel." I sounded tougher than I felt.

The creature had one short leg, but he took off at a fast trot. I hurt all over. I wasn't going anyplace.

The sun rose, beating down on me. I heard a sound. The creature with the yellow eyes was back with something in his mouth. He dropped a mess of grasshoppers by my paws.

I poked them.

"Eat it," he said. "ABC!"

This was no time for him to start saying the alphabet. "ABC?" I asked.

"Already Been Chewed. I couldn't find a mouse. It's how my mom and dad used to feed me when I was a pup."

It's rude not to eat a gift. They felt crunchy, but they weren't half bad—a little like peanuts. I felt better.

"Are you a coyote?" I asked.

"You're a dog," he said, making it sound like a put-down.

"I'm Cleo—named for a queen."

"I'm Tricky—named for a god."

"Yeah right," I said. "Well, Tricky, thanks for the chow. But I've got to find my way back to my owner."

"Owner," sniffed Tricky. "A human." He lifted his front paw. It was cut off at the end. "From one of his traps," he said. "I almost died. Your owner killed my mother and father too."

"Not my owner," I said. "We're from New York."

The sky changed. I heard thunder. I hate thunder. The rain came down like it was being shot from a fire hose. I shook the water off my back. "I thought that it didn't rain in the desert."

Tricky grinned, like the desert was one big practical joke. I was beginning to think it was. "Follow me," he said. "I'll take you back to your *owner*." We climbed on a ledge little more than a few inches wide. My stomach felt queer, and I don't think it was the grasshoppers. I tried not to look down.

The ground rumbled under my paws. "You don't have subways here, do you?" I asked Tricky. It certainly sounded like a subway.

Tricky's yellow eyes narrowed. He shoved me hard. I growled at him. I may be a little dog, but I don't like to be pushed around.

Suddenly a wall of red mud tumbled down into the canyon.

"Flash flood," said Tricky. Red ooze was pouring past us like ketchup. If Tricky hadn't shoved me, I would be dead now.

We were in a tiny
cave. "What is this place?" I asked.

"Humans used to live here," said Tricky.
"Hundreds of years ago—ones who
thought coyotes were gods."

My fur was matted down from the rain.
I shivered. "It's not good to get cold," said
Tricky softly. He curled his body, making
a space for me. I tucked in close to him.

"Tell me a story?" he asked. He
sounded like a little kid. I told the story
about the time the New York Mets won
the World Series long ago. People were so
happy that giant pretzels rained down
from the sky—pretzels so big that I could
hardly eat a whole one.

"Now tell me a coyote story."

"Do you see those stars?" asked Tricky, lifting his head. "The Coyote god was given a jar full of stars to carry and was told not to lift the lid. But coyotes are born to snoop, and so Coyote peeked inside. All the stars rushed out. Coyote caught the stars and stuck them in the sky. Some of the stars didn't stick. They're still falling back to earth. That's why we have shooting stars. And one of the falling stars burned Coyote's nose."

"So that's why all coyotes and dogs have a black nose," I said, licking his nose.

We fell asleep in that cave.

When we awoke, I saw a double rainbow. It ended on the ridge, where I knew Martin was looking for me, scared and worried.

"Tricky?" I asked. "Why were you howling last night?"

Tricky looked away. "I was lonely after my mom and dad were killed," he mumbled under his breath.

I licked my lips. "I know what it's like to be alone," I said.

"You," sniffed Tricky. "You've got your owner to love."

"I don't love all humans," I said. "Martin gave me a home when no one wanted me. He loves me."

"Follow me," said Tricky, but he already sounded lonesome.

We climbed more easily now. We watched our rainbow fade.

Tricky's ears twitched when we reached the top. Martin was running toward us, calling "Cleo, Cleo!"

Suddenly Lou lifted the gun to his shoulder. Tricky was a perfect target. I bounded for Lou. I pounced, my paws hitting Lou in the chest, knocking him backward.

I licked Martin. Then I trotted back to Tricky. "You'd better go," I said.

"Come with me," said Tricky.

"Come on, Cleo," shouted Martin's mom.

Tricky turned his back on me. I watched him go.

The sky was pink, but underneath the pink it was full of stars thrown every which way by the Coyote god.

I tipped my head back. *Ow-woo-ooooooo-owoooooooo!* Mine was a howl from the streets.

Across the canyon, Tricky tipped his head until it almost touched his back. *Ow-woo-ooooooo-owooooooo!*

Our howls bounced off the canyon walls. A coyote does know about love.

I first saw Diana Bryer's wonderful paintings on cards that I found when I was traveling in the West. By an amazing coincidence my editor, Katherine Brown Tegen, had also seen her cards and had encouraged Diana to try her hand at children's books.

In a second and almost spooky coincidence, my own dog, Gingy, looks a lot like Diana's wonderful drawings of Cleo.

I had a chance to listen to coyotes when I was on a mountain bike trip in Utah. It rained so much that our whole group got stuck in the mud. It was the most rain that area had received in three days in over a hundred years. The rain gave me lots of time to think up stories as I listened to the coyotes and sat in my leaky tent. But this book is about more than stray dogs and coyotes. I think it is about how we all may hate to be "owned," yet we all long to love and belong to someone.

—E.L.

Diana Bryer, Elizabeth Levy, and friend.